J
KESEY, Ken
The sea lion

A

DATE DUE

KEN KESEY

THE SEA LION

A story of the Sea Cliff People

ILLUSTRATED BY

NEIL WALDMAN

VIKING

VIKING
Published by the Penguin Group
Viking Penguin, a division of Penguin Books USA Inc.,
375 Hudson Street, New York, New York 10014, U.S.A.
Penguin Books Ltd, 27 Wrights Lane, London W8 5TZ, England
Penguin Books Australia Ltd, Ringwood, Victoria, Australia
Penguin Books Canada Ltd, 2801 John Street,
Markham, Ontario, Canada L3R 1B4
Penguin Books (N.Z.) Ltd, 182–190 Wairau Road,
Auckland 10, New Zealand

Penguin Books Ltd, Registered Offices:
Harmondsworth, Middlesex, England

First published in 1991 by Viking Penguin,
a division of Penguin Books USA Inc.

10 9 8 7 6 5 4 3 2 1

Library of Congress Cataloging-in-Publication Data
Kesey, Ken. The sea lion / Ken Kesey ; illustrated by
Neil Waldman   p.   cm.
Summary: Although taunted for his small size and
bad leg, Eemook proves his worth by saving his tribe
from an evil and powerful spirit that comes visiting
one stormy night.
1. Indians of North America—Northwest, Pacific—
Juvenile fiction. [1. Indians of North America—
Northwest, Pacific—Fiction. 2. Physically
handicapped—Fiction. 3. Magic—Fiction.] I.
Waldman, Neil, ill. II. Title.
PZ7.K4814Se 1991 [Fic]—dc20   90-26146 CIP AC
ISBN 0-670-83916-7

Printed in U.S.A.   Set in 11 point Trump
Art direction and design by Joy Chu

To Katherine Grace,
the First . . .

     —K.K.

To the fawn in the valley
whose eyes of golden light
once shone upon me.

     —N.W.

OUR STORY this time is not so much about Princess Shoola as about her friend, Eemook, and how he dealt with the strange spirit that came one night to entrance the Sea Cliff People.

The boy Eemook was the Sea Cliff tribe's spoonmaker. This job was usually assigned to one of the old people who could be better spared to crawl about on the beach, scavenging for shells. It was not the proper task for a young brave.

But Eemook was a cripple, as well as the son of an Um-Onono—meaning "Slave Woman." Um-Onono had been captured as a child when the Sea Cliff People still made raids on the Copper People, far to the south. Like Eemook, it had been her lot in life to do the tasks none of the others wanted. On the day that Eemook was to be born, his mother had been gathering sea urchins from a dangerous tide pool. Without warning, a sly wave caught her from behind.

The wave carried her to the cliff rocks and mauled her cruelly. When it was done it cast her up on the beach with the driftwood. The netsmen pulled her from the surf and pounded the water from her lungs. When her breath began, so did her labor. After the child was born, the unfortunate young mother died on the pebbles, barely a woman.

Her death left her poor offspring nothing but a cocked backbone and a shrunken leg. Chief Gawgawnee decided at once that the baby should be left on the low rocks, the way the girl babies were often disposed of.

"It will be best to send this broken moonfawn along with the doe that bore it," the chief maintained. "Let the Sea Spirits finish what they have begun."

Most of the People agreed. But Um-Lalagic, the ancient root woman, who slept alone because she was barren and produced only foul winds, spoke up for the babe:

"I shall keep him," she said. "I shall raise him and make him strong with clam nectar and honey. I shall call him Eemook, The Broken Gift, and he shall call me Grandmother. If you do

not do this thing for me," she told the chief, her eyes sharp as flint, "I shall take the Long Walk with him myself. I swear it."

So Chief Gawgawnee took back his sentence and told the old woman that she could keep the child. In truth, he was swayed more by Um-Lalagic's ability as child watcher than root finder. Her skill at the shadow drum had quieted many an annoying crybaby in the longhouse.

Some of the clan muttered against the chief's change of mind; they claimed that the spirits were often known not to favor unsteady leaders, or deformed orphans, either.

The old woman paid the mutterers no heed. She raised the boy in her corner of the longhouse and protected him with her flinty glare. She worked hard to coax his shrunken leg to grow. She rubbed his back with special oils and sang many healing chants. But his bones never straightened. With his walking stick he could keep up with the smaller of the boys; without the stick he could only move himself along in a kind of floundering hop, like something from a bog.

Still, as though to make up for these defects, the Great Giver-and-Watcher had also given Eemook long, smart fingers, and a tongue clever at story singing, and sharp, proud eyes like Oorvek the Osprey, who can circle higher than the sun and still see the perfect twig to finish the nest.

Young Eemook had always been satisfied enough with these gifts. He liked making spoons. He didn't mind that boys younger than his years were already out on the rocks, assisting the spearmen. Sometimes Shoola slipped away to keep him company; and when she didn't there were always the little animals that crept out of the rocks and bushes to join him. So he had attended to his solitary task over many long seasons, cheerfully and without complaint; and he was happy.

But one fall afternoon this all changed. . . .

He was on the beach beneath the grassy bluff, at the big smooth stone where he did his work. The waves were quiet. He had already scavenged the high waterline to see what last night's tide had brought in. There wasn't much; the sea had been calm for many weeks, too lazy to stir up anything interesting.

Eemook knew this was soon to change. It was late in the season. The drooping sun showed the bellies of many clouds swelling to the north. Eemook was busy with his bow drill, making holes in the shells he had collected so the notched handles could be tied securely. When he would raise his eyes from his work he could see the other men on the rocks, intently hunting the foamy currents. They could sense the coming change, as well. They danced from rock to rock with their young helpers, holding their three-pointed spears high, singing as they danced. They were singing their wish for the one last prize they each hoped to capture before the gathering season ended.

The women also sang, hurrying back and forth along the path above with their baskets on their shoulders.

As he watched the men and women singing and working together, Eemook began to feel sad. He pictured how he must look to them, propped against the distant stone. For the first time in his life he saw how small he really was—how inferior—and it made him very, very lonely. He found himself wishing he also had a helper to sing and work with. He was hoping his playmate Shoola might slip away and come and help him hold the shells for his drilling, when, as if in response to his wish, he heard his name called:

"Yi, Eemook, yi!"

It was the princess herself. She had stepped from the path to wave to him. Her cedar skirt was tucked high and her long hair was flapping about her shoulders, like the blue-black wings of the raven. She was waving her basket to him so he could see. It was a woman's basket; the weavers had presented it to her that very morn.

Eemook waved back, clacking his bow and bit together above his head. As he was waving, Shoola's father, Chief Gawgawnee, came blustering along, wrapped in his royal robes and fat. He saw Eemook waving to his daughter.

"You worthless jellyfish!" the chief shouted. "You crippled slaveboy *frog!* You do no worthy work and you offer no respect to your superiors. You do not even know how to be a good slave. Spoonmaker? Paw! You would make better crab bait."

It was not true that he did no worthy work, but respect had never been an easy offering for Eemook to make—especially to

this blubber-faced old blusterer. For this reason the boy had suffered many harsh scoldings and beatings. But his proud eyes never lowered. Even now he glared back at Chief Gawgawnee, reaching as he did for a piece of driftwood.

The chief took a quick step back. For all the little slave's handicaps, it was well known that Eemook had very strong arms and a history of hurling things when angered—with alarming accuracy!

"Shoola! All of you dawdling girls! Ignore this frogboy slave! Back to work, back to work."

The chief blustered on, shooing his daughter and the others ahead of him, over the slopes . . . leaving the disrespectful orphan behind in the little cove.

The waves went quieter still. The barnacles clicked and the mussels hissed. The wind cried its mournful cry in the ribbon grass—"Lonely . . . O, loneleee-e-e." Eemook's eyes filled in sympathy with that wind. He felt smaller and lonelier than ever. At length, he put aside his drill and bit and spoke out loud to himself:

"I do not wish to be a frog boy forever," he said. "I wish . . . I wish I could *change.* I wish that at least I could turn into a frog *man!*"

What he truly wished, though, was that Shoola would come keep him company again, the way she used to. Perhaps the two wishes were the same wish. He did not know. He did know that neither wish was very likely to come true. Shoola was the chief's only living child. Though Chief Gawgawnee had fathered many offspring, they had all been girl babies, and at his practical com-

mand their cradle had been that cruel surf at the bottom of the big cliff. But on the day that Shoola was born it happened that the chief had enjoyed an exceptionally fine day at his fishing weir. Forty red salmon and a fat seal calf in the stone maze! The chief ventured that perchance this new baby might be the bringer of such good fortune, so he called her Shoola, Luck Bringer, and let his wives keep her.

Eemook and Shoola were the only children of that season. Shoola grew to be Eemook's only true friend, and he hers. Now she was gathering with the women, with her skirt tucked high. Eemook looked at his own bare legs.

"This wishing will change nothing," he sighed. "While a tadpole can become a frog, a frog will never turn into anything more than a frog. Things are what they were made to become."

He set his jaw and bent back to the bow. As the twine whined and the drill spun, he heard the men singing on the rocks. The chant they sang was a song of praise of the sea. It called the sea an adversary that should be ever battled, a "Great Warrior" from whom the victories of food must be won.

The women hurrying along with their baskets of crabs and clams—and sea grasses and fern root to grind for the People's bread—sang back. Their song claimed that the sea was a Mighty Mother that should be feared for her ferocity, and honored for the care and nourishment she granted her children.

"The sea is neither a Great Warrior nor a Mighty Mother," Eemook said to himself. "The sea is nothing but a great bowl of fish stew! And I, Eemook, shall honor it as a spoonmaker should—with a great big *spoon*."

And with that he reached into the bottom of his basket and took out a roll of woven cedar. After looking both ways he began to unroll the bundle. From the wrapping he produced a gleaming wonder—a carved bone, ivory white and gently curved, like the slimmest crescent of the newest moon . . . and longer than the boy's good leg!

It was the rib of some colossal beast. Eemook had discovered it after a storm, long ago, and he had carved it secretly over many seasons. No one had ever seen it, not even Shoola. Eemook had fashioned the length of the white crescent into all the little animals he had come to know and love in his lonely life: the sand runner and the shy rock crab; the tree peeper and the pine squirrel and the puffin. All the denizens of the cliffs and shore were perfectly entwined down the length of his creation, each flowing into the other and linking firm, like links of a living chain.

The hilt of the bone was already drilled and slotted where

the big shell must fit. Eemook had been watching for such a shell almost from the day he had discovered the great bone. He had never found anything nearly large or beautiful enough. Or perfect enough.

"But the longer the wait," he said to cheer himself up, "the more perfect my little family will become!"

And he set to polishing the intricate creatures with wet sand and moss, singing as he worked:

> Here I have a chain, of family I think
> They link! They link! They link! They link!
> Each to each, each to other
> The frog to the mouse to the weasel . . .
> And they wait. They wait! They wait! They wait!
> To find the great shell to make the great vessel
> Then they will shine together ah *hee!*
> Like the Spoon of Stars that wheels
> About the Star That Never Moves.
> Ah *hee* hi yi! Ah *hee* hi family family family.

His spirits lifted as he worked. So intent on his singing and shining did he become that he did not notice the girl, Shoola. The young princess had come down from the path after all. She was creeping down the little cliff behind him, her basket full of sea grass and her eyes bright with mischief. Closer and closer she crept, until she was right behind him. Then, with a wild laugh, she dumped all the wet brown grasses over Eemook's head!

When he saw who it was that had tricked him, Eemook lunged, standing with a shout. He tried to catch his friend, but of course she was too nimble. She danced out of his reach around the big rock, laughing and pointing. When Eemook saw the shape his shadow made on the sandy cliff, he laughed also; the sea grasses hung down his shoulders like the mane of some ragged animal. Laughing, he fell to his all-fours and began to rock his head to and fro, mooing, like the little rock-seal bull mooing its song of courtship to a young seal heifer.

"Hah-*moooo*," he mooed, "I am the Dancer of the *Deep*. I will dance you into sleep, I will take you to my keep . . . Hah-*moo-o-o!*"

The girl shrieked with delight and fell to her knees to join her playmate. She shook her hair down over her face.

"Not *me-e-e!*" she chanted back. "I am fast and free. I won't sleep beneath your sea . . ."

Thus were the two friends chanting and rocking when the boy's grandmother, Um-Lalagic, came along the path from her root gathering. For a moment she was filled with fear by what she beheld on the beach below. When she saw it was only Shoola and Eemook, her fear changed to anger. She began to throw the unwashed roots down on them.

"Foolish children," she scolded. "Scornful, disrespectful children! Would you mock the spirits? *Tshh!* Very foolish! Very dangerous and foolish!"

"It is only play, Grandmother," Eemook called back.

"Then it is foolish play, even for children. Stop at once and get back to your tasks. And *hurry*. For I have just heard that this is the last day of fall. Winter is on its way this very minute."

"And where did you hear this from, Old Grandmother?" Shoola asked with an innocent smile. "Perhaps from one of the 'Little Winds?' " The princess had always enjoyed teasing the old root finder about her bloated condition.

"More mockery!" Um-Lalagic screeched. "Mockery and scorn!"

She tossed more roots. Shoola squealed and took shelter beneath her basket. For an old woman, Um-Lalagic had a very keen throwing hand. It was she who had taught Eemook. She finally ceased her barrage, breathing hard:

"If you must know, you wicked girl . . . I heard it from Tasalgic the Crow. He told me that storms will strike this *very night. Bad* storms. Look—" She pointed to the mountains. "See those pine tops dancing in the purple clouds? Tasalgic told me that's how it would begin. The Sea Cliff People must finish gathering this very day, or there will be many loud bellies in the longhouse before next season. So make haste! And no more mockery."

As soon as the old woman waddled away up the hill toward the longhouse, Shoola burst anew into laughter. "That crow is a famous liar," she said. "And that root woman's belly is loud in *any* season."

Eemook laughed along. The People had always joked about the nether noises of old Um-Lalagic, calling her Root Rumbler or Bladder Sack. Or Spider Squaw—for indeed she did look like a spider with her skinny limbs and her big belly. But Eemook loved the old woman and knew that for all her growling and wind breaking she was very wise, and he set about helping Shoola refill her basket.

When the last tangle of grasses was lifted from the stone, there lay the beautiful bone. Eemook had forgotten his carving in the play. He tried to roll it from sight, back in the cloth, but the girl begged to see it.

"Have I ever," she asked somberly, "in all our lives, kept from you even one secret?"

He knew she had not. Slowly he unfolded the wrapping.

"Oh, Eemook!" she exclaimed, "it is a *handle* . . . the grandest I have ever seen! Never has anyone carved a more wonderful spoonhandle! But *where* will you ever find the shell to finish it? There is no such shell in all the sea."

Eemook was so proud he could hardly answer. "My grandmother says . . . that for every hook there is a fish; and for every spade a hole. Something will come."

He started to return the carving to its wrapping, but Shoola stopped him.

"I must hold it, Eemook," she begged. "For only a little while?"

Eemook was reluctant. No other hand had ever touched it. The magic might leak out. "Yes, you may look at it," he said at last, "but I must hold to one end."

He held forth the bone and allowed Shoola to run her fingers along its length. As she did this a very strange thing happened. Everything seemed to become very still. The wind stopped and the pine tops became still. All the shoreside bustle ceased as well. The men on the rocks and the women on the bluff went stiff, frozen in their hurry like carved totem poles.

The sea itself was the only thing that had not gone completely still, but it had slowed considerably. The waves rolled as leisurely as summer clouds, and much brighter, though the sky was dark as clay.

And when the two friends squinted out into the brightness, they saw, moving from crest to crest, as though from gentle hand to hand, a gleaming round object, being passed shoreward, slowly . . . carefully . . . until it was laid in the sand at the feet of Princess Shoola.

It was a beautiful shell, larger than any clam or mussel or scallop, larger even than the abalone, and far more brilliant! It was so bright that to look into the center of it made the stomach spin like a whirlpool.

"Oh, Eemook! Your grandmother was right!" the girl cried. "For every footprint there must be a foot."

And so saying she picked up the shell, which was bigger than both her spread hands. It gleamed between the young pair like a pool of moonlight. She held it out for the boy to try to match to the handle. The scalloped rim perfectly fit into the carved notch.

"Now, truly, it is the most wonderful in all the world," Shoola said softly.

Eemook beamed with pride. "The People will be very impressed," he declared. "All the women will gape and pluck at their throats. All the men will say that Eemook is the most marvelous maker of spoons in all the houses on all the shores! Perhaps your father will even stop calling me a worthless slave-boy."

"Perhaps your grandmother will stop pelting me with roots!" Shoola added, joining her friend in his excitement.

"I will present it to the People on the first winter feast. I will bring it forth to dip from the Feastnight pot! Your father will be very envious."

"Oh!" Shoola cried, suddenly alarmed. "Then you must not show it! For you know my father. If my father envies something he cannot have, he always declares potlatch. Then you would be forced to throw your treasure away."

When a potlatch was declared, each grown member of the tribe had to give up his most prized possession. Potlatch could not be denied; it was a way the Watcher-and-Giver kept the People from growing too proud over each other.

Eemook knew Shoola was right. Whenever one of the men made a better spear than the chief's, the jealous old man declared potlatch; he could always order himself another spear. Yes, the chief would have the marvelous spoon destroyed if he could not possess it.

Then Eemook's eyes brightened.

"We will have our *own* feastnight, here and now, and no fathers or grandmothers. We shall invite all of my family to the feast!" The boy held the curved bone aloft. "They can see how I have honored them with my carving. They will come, one by one, and I will introduce you. I will say, 'Mr. Squirrel, this is Princess Shoola, Bringer of Good Luck, and my lifelong friend. Princess Shoola, this is Mr. Tsick-tsick, the Squirrel!'"

And from behind the rock came the product of their play, a bone-white squirrel with his bushy tail waving and his eyes shining. He bowed gracefully to the girl and she bowed back.

"And this is Miss Loon," Eemook continued. A young loon appeared, wearing a bead necklace. "Miss Loon, please say hello to Shoola, who is also becoming a woman."

"You are very beautiful," the loon said.

"And you," Shoola said, blushing.

"And this is Mr. Ouzle . . . and this is Mrs. Puffin . . ."

One after another the creatures appeared and joined the young couple in their fancy, dancing around them in the sand. As they danced, the boy's leg straightened and the crook released its lock on his back. He threw aside his pine cane and joined the dance. Round and round the rock they all danced, hand in paw in fin in wing.

They danced for what seemed hours; and the hours might have become days if Tasalgic the Crow had not suddenly swooped down from the dark sky, cawing an ominous warning.

"Storm claw!" the black bird called at the dancers. "Bad storm claw! Claw! Claw!"

No sooner had he passed than a furious flash of lightning shattered the children's fantasy. The animals vanished. The wind was once more whipping the pines. A towering wave smashed the rocks and sent the men scurrying up the cliff with their spears. The women again rushed to gather the last of the fish from the drying racks.

"This time that lying crow was speaking the truth," Shoola shouted against the wind. "Winter has indeed arrived."

Eemook grabbed up his tools and stick and hurried for the footholes cut in the cliff. Shoola hurried to get her new basket. Stinging hail began to pelt down. Eemook had reached the top of the bluff before he suddenly remembered their wonderful prize. He could see the shell, gleaming like a little moon on the beach stone below.

"Shoola!" he shouted against the rising gale. "The shell! The shell!"

The girl leaped back to the beach but a second giant wave was already rolling toward the big stone. When it rolled back the girl was drenched and the stone swept bare. The sea that had so gently bestowed the gift had just as cruelly reclaimed it.

NSIDE THE LONGHOUSE there was a tempest almost as furious as the one outside. All was confusion and turmoil and last-minute frenzy to batten the holes and windows against the storm. The fire maker was building up the center fire as fast as he could break sticks. Blue smoke swirled and billowed. The small children were hugging each other in fright, and the big children's eyes were big when the lightning flashed through the cracks in the cedar planks.

The fire was beginning to roar when, suddenly, the chief held up his hands.

"Where is Shoola?" he demanded. "Where is my daughter?"

"And Eemook?" the old grandmother cried. "My little Eemook, where is he?"

"Perhaps the tide has finally reclaimed the slaveboy," said one of the chief's wives. "And our poor daughter in the bargain."

Just then there was a pounding on the big door of the longhouse. The men rushed to undo the thongs. The young couple staggered in, drenched and gasping.

"Troublesome toad!" the chief cursed, kicking Eemook. "You will be the poison of us all!" He kicked Eemook all the way to the darkest end of the longhouse where his grandmother wrapped him in a blanket.

When the door was once again lashed fast and the cracks caulked, the preparations for the evening's meal resumed. The heating stones were dug from the firepit and dropped steaming into the cooking pots. The women began to grind the roots and fish eggs together on the family stones to make their cakes. The men smoked and rocked on their hunkers. The old grandmother chanted her soothing songs to calm the tempest without.

But the chants went unheeded. The storm grew wilder. The wind began to shake the house so terribly that all the children, little or big, were soon crying and calling their mothers from the cooking.

"Make a show, Wind Widow," the chief commanded. "Quiet these puppies! What are you here for?"

So the old grandmother arranged her oil lamp to cast a bright beam against the elk-bladder drum. She began to make shadow figures with her hands, singing as she did:

Then *here* is the chick,
The child of the sandpiper,
Lost on the beach, crying in the storm
Afraid of the wind, of the terrible sea . . .
"Ai-yee! Ai-yee! What will become of me? Of mee-e-e?"

The frightened children quieted a little. They began to creep toward the old grandmother's show. Her dancing figures produced another shadow:

Now *here* is the mother piper,
Circling down, down from the blue
To spread her wings over her child, piping
"Kee-loo! Kee-loo! Nothing will happen to you!
To you!"

The wind outside seemed to quiet a little as well. The children settled down around the old woman. The mothers resumed their chores. At the firepit Shoola had removed her doeskin blouse and was drying her hair. When she looked up and saw Eemook watching she smiled and tossed her head as she had on the beach. Eemook blushed and turned quickly away to watch the shadow show.

Now *here* is the otter pup
Tossed in the storm's terrible eye
"Ei-yi! Ee-yi! I will drown, and die! And die!"

A larger shade came bobbing along:

Now *here* comes Mother Otter.
"Climb on my breast. Ride to our den.
It is warm and safe, within! Within!"

The children all laughed to see the small shadow leap to the tummy of the larger and go bobbing away. The fear was ebbing away also.

The grandmother had just started to make the next shadow creature when, to the astonishment of all, another loud banging was heard at the longhouse door—*Boom! Boom! Boom!*

Everyone stared. All the tribe was inside; who could it be, outside in this fury? The banging continued, but no one moved. *Boom boom boom! Boom boom boom!* All eyes gradually turned to the chief. Finally the fat chief cleared his throat and called at the booming door.

"Who is there, booming in the night? Speak!"

"A traveler," the answer came back, in a voice polite but deep with echo, as from a cave. "A simple traveler, seeking shelter and a bit of food."

"Do we know you?" the chief called.

"I am a stranger."

"How do we know you are not an enemy?"

The chief motioned for one of his wives to hand him his fish spear from the wall.

"How do we know you are only one and not a tribe of enemies, come to take our winter's store and our women? How do we know what tribe you are? How do we—"

Before the chief could finish the question or the voice make an answer, a mighty gust of wind broke the latch and blew the door wide. A thundering flash revealed the stranger, standing silhouetted, as tall as the big doorway itself.

"I am my own tribe," the silhouette said, and stepped over the threshstone into the light of the firepit.

All the Sea Cliff People gaped at this apparition, spellbound, especially the women. For he was majestically handsome. His eyes were green and his hair gold and he was taller by a head than the tallest of the tribe—and clothed like a king! He was wrapped from shoulder to foot in a long robe of fur that was the same rich color as his hair. On his forehead sat a peaked fur cap studded with stones that glittered more brightly than any the tribe had ever seen. On his wrists and ankles rattled bracelets shinier even than those of the Copper Clan. But most impressive by far was the amulet that hung around the stranger's neck, like the moon on a beaded leash.

Eemook gasped when he saw it. It was the great shell they had found on the beach! It could be no other. He glanced quickly to Shoola to see if his friend recognized the shell. But her face showed that she was as spellbound as the rest of the women by this wondrous stranger with his royal garments and his long, glowing mane. Eemook began to have bad feelings about this visitation.

"I beg only a bit of food," the stranger said, his sea-green eyes darting about the longhouse at the young women. "If your maids can spare a few scraps—?"

Shaking himself from his amazement, the chief ordered the young women to give the visitor all he could eat. He asked if there was anything else he wanted.

"Only a bit of hard floor, perhaps," the stranger said, his eyes still dancing from face to blushing face, "to sleep on."

"And a soft maid to share it with, I warrant," the old woman muttered from her shadowy nook at the other end of the longhouse. Eemook saw that his grandmother did not feel at all good about this intruder, either.

Though she barely whispered, the stranger overheard. He turned straight to the old woman, his eyes blazing. She met his gaze, and for a moment the air between them crackled and smelled of flint. Then, without a word to the chief or anyone else, the man began walking down the longhouse toward the old Um-Lalagic.

"—So, Grandmother," he said, "I see you have a lamp and drumskin. Do you make shadow dances?"

"Sometimes," she growled. "During stormy times, to soothe the children."

"Make for us a dance, then," he bade her. "We will see if there is magic in your shades."

"*Tsssh!*" she hissed. "Who are you to order me? I am not your squaw!"

But the chief called to her, "Do as he commands, Dung Sack. Any eye can see this brave is of royal blood, perhaps a chieftain king. Obey him."

Reluctantly, the old woman turned back to the light from the lamp. "Then *here* then," she chanted, "is the frog . . . jumping and singing because the rain does not worry him. 'Jum-bump, Jum-bump.' Because the rain does not trouble him—"

"Then *here* then," the stranger interrupted, casting his own hand shadow on the drumskin, "is the salamander that *swallows* the frog. 'Ga-lup, Ga-lup,' and *nothing* troubles the frog."

The frog disappeared into the jaws of the lizard. The children all applauded with glee and the people laughed. Eemook could tell that his grandmother was not pleased.

"Then *here* then," she sang, "is the big blue heron that swoops down on the salamander. His beak is like a flint arrow. His neck is like a drawn bow. Down he swoops . . . down, down—"

The bill of the shadow bird was cocked to stab the lizard,

but the lizard changed instantly into a bigger shadow, with long teeth and sharp ears, and a bristling tail.

"Then *here* is *Kajortoq*, the Fox," the stranger said, quite pleasantly, "to snap the heron's poor thin neck, kah-*rick!*"

And it was done.

"Then *here*," the old woman hissed, "is *Skree*, the Bobcat, to rip the fox's belly—"

And it was done.

"And *here*," the man countered, "is *Amoroq*, the Wolf, to crush the bobcat's back."

And this, too, was done.

"Very well," the old woman said. "Then *here* then, is the great *she*-bear . . . the great *white* she-bear, from the far white north . . . to slap the wolf's head all the way *off* with her she-bear paws!"

She said this triumphantly, for she knew there was nothing on earth could best the great white she-bear from the north.

The man only smiled. "But *here* then," he said, "is Kawtoolu, the Surf Dragon from the shore across the burning sea—!" and from the darkness he fashioned a huge and awful thing, a creature none of the tribe had seen before, even in their most frightful mushroom sleeps. It had long curving claws and horns all down its spine, and cavernous, yawning, jagged jaws. These jaws opened over the she-bear shadow.

"—Kawtoolu, the Surf Maker, that comes up when the foam is blood-red from a baby girl and gnaws the middle from *all* the bears, black, brown, or white, and leaves behind the empty pelts."

The terrible jaws crumpled the bear shadow.

"And then *here*," he kept on, before the old woman could overcome her shock, "is *Ahk-kharu*, the double-headed Water Omp, who walks the ocean bottom upright like a man and never sleeps, one head awake by day, the other by night. And then *here*, then, is *Tsagag-lalal*, She Who Watches Around Corners with eyes on stalks and has poison in her step like the centipede. And *here* is *Payu*, the Pool Crawler, whose face is rotting entrails and whose outbreathing spawns maggots and whose inbreathing sucks the mocking hearts from little boys that would be men but have not the power . . ."

It seemed to Eemook that these last words were spoken to him, and him alone. When he turned from the drumskin to the man's face, the green eyes were two whirlpools, spinning the boy's stomach, dizzying his head, sucking him down . . . down,

into a deep green chill. When he ceased spinning, Eemook found himself in a forest of waving seaweed. The water was thick, and sad, dark forms swam slowly, this way and that, around a great white throne. The throne was shaped like the shell.

Eemook knew then that this strange visitor was not a human at all, but some kind of God-spirit in a man's body. This cold and silent place was the spirit's domain and the mournful forms were the minions of his court. Somehow Eemook knew as well that he was the only one that perceived this dreadful vision— that the rest of the tribe saw only shadows on elk hide. Why had the stranger revealed this to him alone? Was it because he had mocked the spirits with his play? And why had this being concealed his true identity from the others?

Then he saw the columns of seaweed part, and a huge shaggy beast come swimming toward the throne. It looked as large as Ooma, the Killer Whale. As it swam closer Eemook saw, to his horror, that someone was riding the beast. It was Shoola! Her long hair was waving sluggishly about her bare shoulders and she seemed to be laughing in some kind of dreamy stupor, soundlessly.

"No!" Eemook screamed. "Stop!" The vision evaporated. He was back in the longhouse, at the shadow skin. Everyone was staring at him. "He's not what he seems!"

He struck out with his cane but the stranger stepped aside, laughing. Eemook hopped around to swing again. This time he flopped to the floor, so hard it knocked the breath out of him. He lay there, rolling and gasping.

"I see the frog boy's legs are not properly formed." The

stranger made a shadow of a half-finished frog. "Perhaps he has not properly learned when to get on his knees."

"He will never learn!" the chief exclaimed. "Though he is the whelp of a slave and a cripple to boot, he has *never* shown proper respect!"

"Then, perhaps," the stranger said pleasantly, "his legs will disappear completely."

And the shadow on the drumskin became a tadpole, wriggling helplessly out of water.

Everyone in the longhouse applauded the shadow play. The children squealed with delight and mimicked Eemook's wretched rolling on the floor. All the men puffed and nodded, and the women laughed and pointed and pounded their sides. Even Shoola.

By this time the stew in the chief's cookpot was done. The chief dipped out a bowl, making sure to get the biggest pieces of meat, and handed this bowl to Shoola.

"Give this to our guest," he told the girl. "For it is clear to me that he is not only a great chief but a powerful shaman as well. Our longhouse is honored by his presence."

As she handed the tall stranger the food, he smiled into her face. When Eemook saw how she smiled back at the stranger he felt the basket of his life go empty.

Heartbroken, the crippled spoonmaker slunk back to his corner on his hands and knees. There he found his grandmother behind the shadow screen. She was rocking back and forth on her heels and humming. She was humming the Slow Song, the

chant that old people make when they are ready to take the path to the cliffs for the last time.

"Why is it you that sings the Long Walk, my Grandmother?" the boy asked bitterly. "It is *my* middle that has been gnawed away, not yours. It is *my* seasons that have been emptied, not yours. Why do you wish to end your life?"

The old woman slowly raised her eyes. They no longer twinkled; they were dull and smudged, as though by defeat itself.

"When the house stinks and the chimney is clogged," she said, "it is usually time to get out of the house."

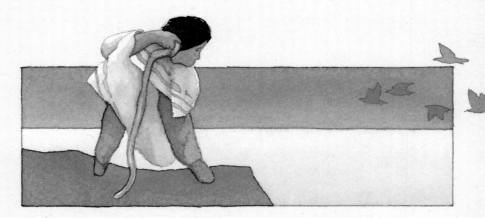

THE STORM PASSED and the longhouse grew still. It was late. The fire in the pit had burned very low and the shadows were long. After the excitement everyone was sleeping deeply. The longhouse was so still it seemed half-empty.

Eemook was still in the corner where he had crawled, his cedar robe drawn over his head. He had not slept all night, so tormented was he by despair. So this was what wishing brought—more bad bargains! He knew now that the pompous old chief was never going to accept him as one of the People. His playmate was never going to be his true mate, any more than his legs were going to turn into true legs. He felt like there was but one way left. His grandmother had hummed this way for him before she dropped into a murmuring sleep. Now it was time. Careful not to awaken the old woman, he slid from beneath the robe. He untied the lashes on the firewood door near their dark corner. He crept through, dragging his basket behind him. He hobbled through the mist until he found the dark path to the cliffs.

He could hear the sea ahead of him, snoring softly between the tides. The full moon strove to part the last of the storm clouds and some stars could be seen. As he walked an owl swooped near his head and perched in a pine top, calling. "Go you? Go you . . . ?" Eemook knew the meaning of the owl's call.

"Yes, kind bird of the night," Eemook answered. "This is my Long Walk and you may sing my song. I have no heart left to do it myself."

The owl was still singing when Eemook reached the big cliff.

The boy closed his eyes and wrapped his arms about his basket of tools and carvings, waiting for the owl to finish. The sea crooned from the dark rocks below. He stepped to the edge. But just then he heard another sound, coming from back toward his little beach. It was a strange muffled bellowing sound, like the voice of something neither beast nor man nor spirit, but something struggling between all three. Eemook hobbled through the grass to the bluff and beheld a fearful sight.

There on the beach lay all the tribe's maidens, tumbled on the sand in sodden sleeps, like piles of wet rags. All of them! Rocking on the sand in silent trances! No wonder the longhouse had seemed half-empty.

The only girl not wet was Shoola. Though she was on her feet, she appeared to be as much entranced as the others. Like one who has eaten the speckled mushroom, she was walking across the moonlit sand—her skirt tucked high and her arms held wide. Her eyes were fixed straight ahead, like a baby transfixed by the lamplight. But this light came from no candlefish oil wick; it came from the throat of a shaggy hulk—the very monster Eemook had seen in his spinning vision! The glow was made by the shell! The enchanted shell! Swaying back and forth at the shaggy throat, as the big creature rocked from side to side in the shallow surf.

And poor, beautiful, transfixed Shoola was about to straddle the monster for a ride in the waves! The other girls were already nearly drowned. It had saved her for last.

With another shout of outrage Eemook started for the sandstone steps. The monster's head swung. When it saw the boy it bellowed with amusement. But Eemook knew better than to repeat the impetuous attack he had made in the longhouse. Balancing on one leg he hurled his pine cane, as the grandmother had hurled her roots. It struck the monster, butt first, on the side of his hairy neck. The thing bellowed again, but not with amusement. Then Eemook snatched the adz from his basket and threw it with all his might. It struck the monster full on the nose. Eemook hurled his heavy stone hammer and heard it thump hard against the creature's ribs. This time when the monster roared it reached up to touch the swaying shell with its

flipper. It reared upright and its hairy mane fell away. As Eemook watched, the monster turned into the stranger, standing naked save for the shell glowing about his neck. Bellowing, the giant started for the sandstone steps.

The only other heavy thing that Eemook had to throw was his carved rib. He pulled it from his bag. The stranger appeared to hesitate. Eemook raised it above his head and the stranger retreated back down the steps. Eemook could feel the carving throb with power.

Back on the beach, the man turned to the enthralled maidens. "Go!" he bellowed. "Chase him! Catch him! Rip him apart! We will feed the pieces to the crabs."

The girls came up the bluff, howling.

Using the bone for his cane, Eemook turned and fled for the forest, running as he never had run before in his life. The carving not only supported him, it seemed to guide him in the dark—behind this rock! Beneath that huckleberry! The girls came on like a pack of wolves, but they could not catch him for all their strong young legs. And the farther from the sea they pursued him, the less they howled. As the chase wore on, one by one the maids stopped, and turned, and began to drift back toward the longhouse. In silence, like dreamwalkers.

Shoola was the last to leave. From the hollow stump where he hid, Eemook listened to her thrashing in the salal nearby. She was whimpering in confusion. Once he thought he heard her whisper his name, but he did not move.

When she was gone he lay back in the wooden bowl while his breathing slowed. He looked at the circle of sky above. The clouds parted and the moon came down and shone into his eyes, which were going sharp and hard, like the eyes of Oorkek, the Sea Eagle, when she is angry.

I N THE LONGHOUSE all was still with the approach of dawn. The maidens were tucked again in their family robes as though they had never moved. The men were snoring in ignorance. The stranger was seated on the chief's painted treasure box as though he already owned it. He was wrapped tightly in his long robe, facing the longhouse door.

No one else was awake in the longhouse, except the old grandmother. When the stranger came in she had awakened and resumed her gloomy chant. She rocked to and fro as she hummed, glaring at the stranger's back. He paid her no mind. He continued to watch the door, waiting. Very likely he was expecting more soldiers from his army of shades, she thought. *Tssh!* She no longer cared. Her time was over. She was old. Her magic skill with the shadow play had been her only value for a long time now, and now that magic was smashed. Soon, she would be smashed as well. She rocked harder and knotted her face to hum louder, but a sudden banging froze the breath in her throat.

Boom! Boom! Boom! something boomed at the big door. All the braves sprang to their feet and leapt for their spears. The

maidens held each other, shivering. *Boom! Boom! Boom!* and the door boomed wide.

It was Eemook. He was beating the door with the great carved bone. He hopped into the startled house, dragging his basket and singing. He was singing the Potlatch Song:

> Then *here* is the finish, here at last!
> Here is potlatch! Here is the leveler!
> The torch on the grass,
> The toadstool on the carrion,
> The sprout on the grave.
> Come high and low, come empty or full,
> Come rich or poor or servant or slave
> *Here* is potlatch, for one and all—
> Into the firepit and gone for good.

He snatched his bow drill from the basket and flung it into the firepit. Sparks leaped and the fire began to blaze.

He took out his flint-tipped drills and clacked them together:

> Then *here* are my tools,
> My third and fourth hands—
> *Into* the firepit and gone for good.

A puff of sparks welcomed the shafts. Eemook dug again into his basket.

Then *here* are my spoons and dippers and cups
Spoons, spoons, that were to be.
Spoons for men and women and all—
Into the firepit and gone for good.

By this time the people were all crying out that he reconsider. These were utensils—needed for the winter ahead. "Stop!" shouted Gawgawnee, the chief. "You cannot do this!" But Eemook continued to fling his creations into the fire.

"What is this?" the golden-haired stranger demanded. "What is he doing?"

"The fool is trying to declare *potlatch*," the chief explained in an angry voice. "It means nothing. Only a man who has a great treasure to sacrifice can do such a thing. Stop, slaveboy! You waste our goods . . ."

The young man hopped out of the chief's reach and began tossing his carved dolls into the fire:

Then *here* is the pineknot beaver
With real beaver teeth for the scraping of bowls.
And the drinking duck with agates for eyes—
Into the fire and *into* the fire, and see?
There *is* no other man like Eemook,
There *is* no other man like me . . .

The boy tossed in the empty basket. Now nothing was left

but the carved rib bone. When he held it aloft, all the People were indeed impressed. They saw the little animals shimmer and twist with life in the leaping firelight.

> Now *here* is my treasure—
> Who has carved better?
> From antler or cedar, from bone or wood?
> *Into* the firepit and gone for good!
> And *who* is like Eemook? Who is like Eemook?
> Who here is greater? Who? Who?

Once more the chief cried for the young man to desist, but it was too late. The carving he cast into the flames was more wonderful than any the Sea Cliff People had ever seen, and their blood was stirred. With a cry, another young man accepted the challenge. He pulled his leister spear from the soft earth and threw it in after Eemook's treasure—"*Into* the firepit and gone for good!"

Then a netsman cast his net, as though to snare the leaping flames. And a weaver his basket. The chief's own brother set fire to his feathered drum and beat it while it burned. The voice of the tribe rose up to join Eemook in the Potlatch Song:

> Then *here* it is, then *here* it is.
> *Here* is potlatch, here the leveling.
> There *is* no chief. There *is* no brave.
> There *is* no master. There *is* no slave . . .
> Into the firepit, and gone for good!

Soon all the men were dancing around the firepit, each trying to match his neighbor's sacrifice. With a groan the chief removed his woven crown and sadly placed it on the rising fire.

"We must all do it now," he explained to the stranger, "or the Watcher-and-Giver will be angry with us. It is our law."

The stranger reluctantly removed his own peaked headdress and followed the chief's lead. The chief threw in his doeskin boots and the stranger did the same.

The drums pounded, the fire leaped. Soon all the women were weeping and rubbing sand in their hair in grief at the loss of so many prized possessions, and all the men were dancing naked in the firelight.

"Look to our visitor, my chief!" Eemook called. "Shall he not give of *his* treasure?"

The chief saw that the stranger had not removed his magnificent shell amulet.

"You must throw in the necklace," he said. "Every man must throw in his riches—even a chieftain king."

The stranger stopped dancing. "I will not," he said. "It is a trick on me by that cripple. I will not sacrifice my amulet."

The other men stopped dancing. They looked at their chief and the big visitor. The fire showed the anger in their faces.

"You must," the chief told him, "it is the law of the Sea People. You must throw in your treasure or we must throw you from the high cliff."

"I will not," the stranger said again. "I must not and I shall not! I am more powerful than your law."

Some of the People muttered angrily and began to take up

the boiling stones. The stranger raised his fingers to touch the magical shell. From the shadows flickering against the walls came once again his army of dark demons. They advanced on the People, shrieking furiously and waving their claws. The tribesmen fell back in terror, understanding at last that this handsome stranger must be some kind of invading spirit. But Eemook hopped to the pit and drew out a blazing spear. He thrust it into the black form of the Surf Dragon. The creature squealed with pain.

"They are made of shadows!" he called to his tribesmen. "Nothing but shadows. Drive them into the light!"

Grabbing up burning brands the tribe charged the demon army, driving them out the longhouse door into the dawn. One after the other they melted in the morning sun.

Of all the unearthly beings, only the stranger was left when they reached the cliff's edge. He was bellowing like a wild beast and his handsome face was contorted by rage. With stones and torches they forced him to the edge, then over, into the rushing tide below.

With a roar he disappeared beneath the waves, only to surface moments later in his true form as the huge hairy-maned Lion of the Sea. The brilliant shell could still be seen about his neck as he swam away toward the horizon, bellowing his fury and frustration.

The women began to creep down from the longhouse to peer over the edge. Shoola ran to stand by Eemook's side, her eyes full of pride. The spell was broken.

"Oh, Eemook! You saved us from an evil god! You were so

brave and clever." She turned to the chief. "Wasn't he, father? Clever and brave—?"

"Yes," the chief was forced to admit. "He was clever and brave, for a crippled—" The chief paused, feeling the eyes of his tribe upon him. He knew he looked very fat-bottomed and foolish without his beautiful chieftain's robe. He finished his sentence in almost a whisper. "—spoonmaker."

Eemook met the chief's eyes and was silent. A cripple he would always be—things are as they are—but no more a slaveboy.

Some things, not even the Great Giver-and-Watcher can make to be.

Just then, the People heard an approaching chorus of muffled toots and whistles. They looked up to see old Um-Lalagic hurrying down the path. When she reached the cliff she leaned over and spat into the surf below.

"So, my Grandmother," Eemook smiled, "you no longer sing the Long Walk. Perhaps you have decided not to vacate the smoky house—?"

"Sometimes it isn't a bad chimney after all," she huffed. "Sometimes it is only gas."

The following spring all the maidens except for Shoola gave birth to babes covered with golden hair. The chief ordered them thrown into the sea. But they did not drown. No matter how rough the surf, they always bobbed up and swam away, bellowing.

This was the beginning of the Sea Lion People, and they have been bellowing ever since.